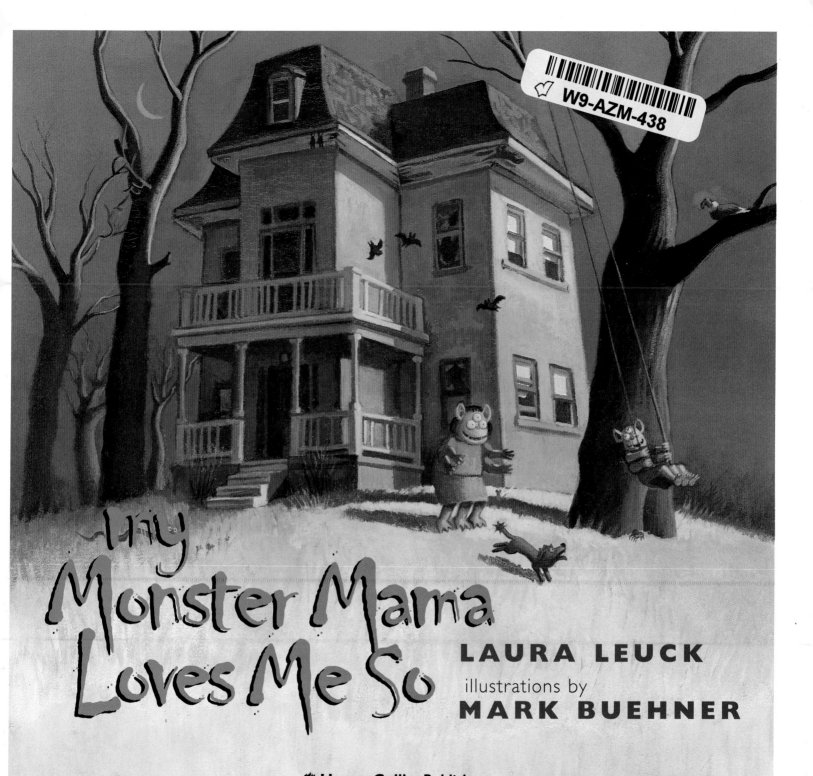

My Monster Mama Loves Me So

LAURA LEUCK

illustrations by

MARK BUEHNER

HarperCollinsPublishers

My monster mama loves me so! Let me tell you how I know.

When I wake up, she tweaks my nose,
tickles all my pointy toes,

combs the cobwebs from my bangs,
and makes sure that I brush my fangs.

She gives me great big hairy hugs,
bakes me cookies filled with bugs,

and when I'm sick she's twice as nice—
she gives me lizard juice with ice.

She helps me climb the jungle gym,

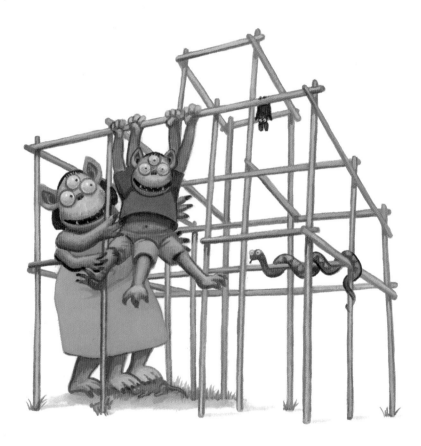

takes me to the swamp to swim,

and comes to all my beastball games.
She claps and stamps and roars my name.

And when the scary things come out
to wave their arms and scream and shout,
she tells me, "Don't be frightened, dear,"
and shows me how to disappear.

On rainy, windy, stormy days,
she breathes and makes a cozy blaze.
We read some books, toss on more logs,
sing camping songs, and roast hot dogs.

On summer evenings after dark
we go strolling through the park.
We practice tricks I've learned today
and gaze up at the Milky Way.

And when the moon sets in the sky,
she sings a monster lullaby
of things that shriek and moan and creep—
soothing things to help me sleep.

She tucks me tightly into bed,
then asks me if my spider's fed
and hangs my favorite bat above me.
That's how I know my mama loves me!

Oops—one other thing is true:
Your monster mama loves you too!

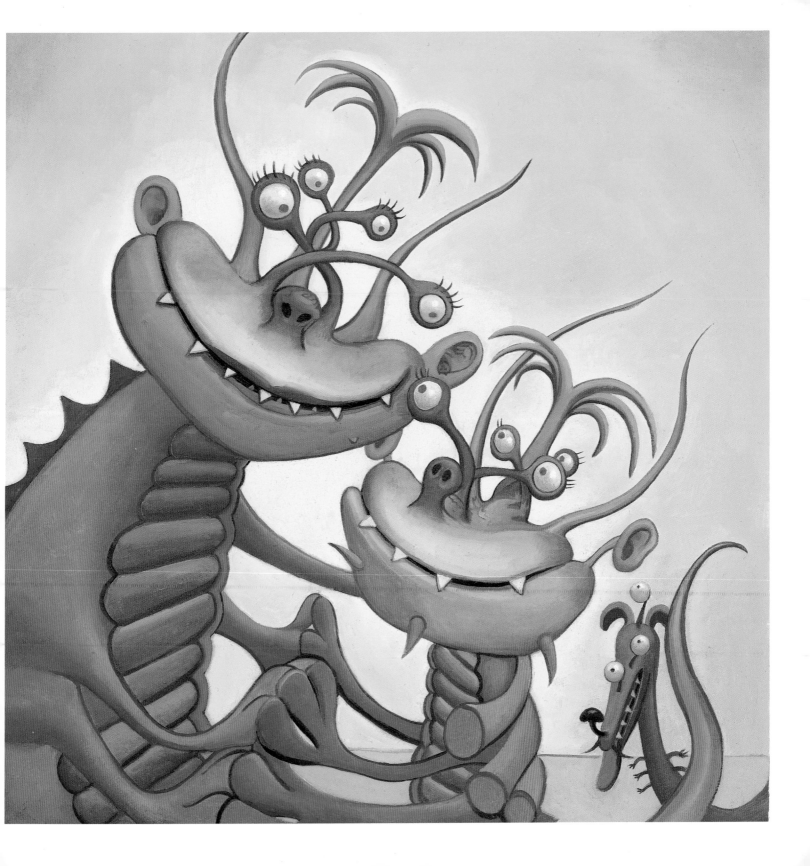

For my husband, Art, with love and thanks
—LL

To my own monster mama
—MB

Acrylic and oil paints were used for the full-color illustrations.
The text type is 16-point Benguiat Gothic.

My Monster Mama Loves Me So
Text copyright © 1999 by Laura Leuck
Illustrations copyright © 1999 by Mark Buehner
Manufactured in China. All rights reserved.

Library of Congress Cataloging-in-Publication Data
Leuck, Laura.
    My monster mama loves me so / by Laura Leuck ; illustrated by Mark Buehner.
        p.   cm.
    Summary: A young monster describes all the things its mother does to show she loves it.
    ISBN 0-688-16866-3 — ISBN 0-688-16867-1 (lib. bdg.)
    ISBN 0-06-008860-5 (pbk.)
    [1. Monsters—Fiction.   2. Mother and child—Fiction.   3. Stories in rhyme.]
I. Buehner, Mark, ill.   II. Title.
PZ8.3.L565Mye   1999   98-48141
[E]—dc21   CIP
                                                        AC

Visit us on the World Wide Web! www.harperchildrens.com